To Kaleb, a world-class drummer and a first-class son. With love, Dad.
– E.O.

For my brother Mark, who loved music.
– K.C.

First Edition
Kane Miller, A Division of EDC Publishing

For information contact:
Kane Miller, A Division of EDC Publishing
PO Box 470663
Tulsa, OK 74147-0663
www.kanemiller.com
www.edcpub.com

Library of Congress Control Number: 2011926767

Manufactured by Regent Publishing Services, Hong Kong
Printed March 2012 in ShenZhen, Guangdong, China

ISBN: 978-1-61067-072-2

1 2 3 4 5 6 7 8 9 10

Dan,
THE TAXI MAN

Written by Eric Ode
Illustrated by Kent Culotta

Here's **Dan,**

Beep! Beep!

THE TAXI MAN...

TAXI
YS
DINER
EMMA
fine
DAN-001

… going to the show and picking up the band.

Climb inside while you still can
with Dan,
Beep! Beep!
the Taxi Man.

TAXI
TAXI
DAN-001

AXI
STOP

STOP!

Here comes Maureen with her tambourine.
Shake-a shake, crash! Shake-a shake, crash!

And here's Dan,
Beep! Beep!
the Taxi Man,
going to the show and picking up the band.

Climb inside while you still can
with Dan,
Beep! Beep!
the Taxi Man.

BEEP
BEEP
TAXI
TAXI
DAN-001

STOP!

Here comes Tyrone with his saxophone.
Squeeba-dee dee, squeeba-dee doo!

Here's Maureen with her tambourine.
Shake-a shake, crash! Shake-a shake, crash!

And here's Dan,
Beep! Beep!
the Taxi Man,
going to the show and picking up the band.

Climb inside while you still can
with Dan,
Beep! Beep!
the Taxi Man.

STOP!

Here comes Star with her electric guitar.
Whee, wazzle, wah! Whee, wazzle, wah!

Here's Tyrone with his saxophone.
Squeeba-dee dee, squeeba-dee doo!

Here's Maureen with her tambourine.
Shake-a shake, crash! Shake-a shake, crash!

And here's Dan,
Beep! Beep!
the Taxi Man,
going to the show and picking up the band.

Climb inside while you still can
with Dan,
Beep! Beep!
the Taxi Man.

U.S.
MAIL

Here comes Clair with her rattly snare.
Rat-a-tat! Rat-a-tat! Rat-a-tat-tat!

Here's Star with her electric guitar.
Whee, wazzle, wah! Whee, wazzle, wah!

Here's Tyrone with his saxophone.
Squeeba-dee dee, squeeba-dee doo!

Here's Maureen with her tambourine.
Shake-a shake, crash! Shake-a shake, crash!

And here's Dan,
Beep! Beep!
the Taxi Man,
going to the show and picking up the band.

Climb inside while you still can
with Dan,
Beep! Beep!
the Taxi Man.

STOP!

Here comes Ace with his upright bass.
Boom, boomba, boom! Boom, boomba, boom!

Here's Clair with her rattly snare.
Rat-a-tat! Rat-a-tat! Rat-a-tat-tat!

Here's Star with her electric guitar.
Whee, wazzle, wah! Whee, wazzle, wah!

Here's Tyrone with his saxophone.
Squeeba-dee dee, squeeba-dee doo!

Here's Maureen with her tambourine.
Shake-a shake, crash! Shake-a shake, crash!

And here's Dan,
Beep! Beep!
the Taxi Man,
going to the show and picking up the band.

Climb inside while you still can
with Dan,
Beep! Beep!
the Taxi Man.

TAXI

STOP!

We're here!

the
ROCK'IN
JOINT

Dan gives a shout, “Everybody out!”

Let's go! Let's go!

Up on the stage;
it's time for the show!

What a place. What a scene!
There's Clair and Ace,
and there's Maureen.
There's Star and Tyrone.

But something's wrong.
There's something missing.
Stop the song!

Star looks around.
"I know what we need.
I know what's missing.
Yes, indeed!"

It's **Dan,**

Beep! Beep!

THE TAXI MAN.

It's **Dan,**

Beep! Beep!

THE TAXI MAN.